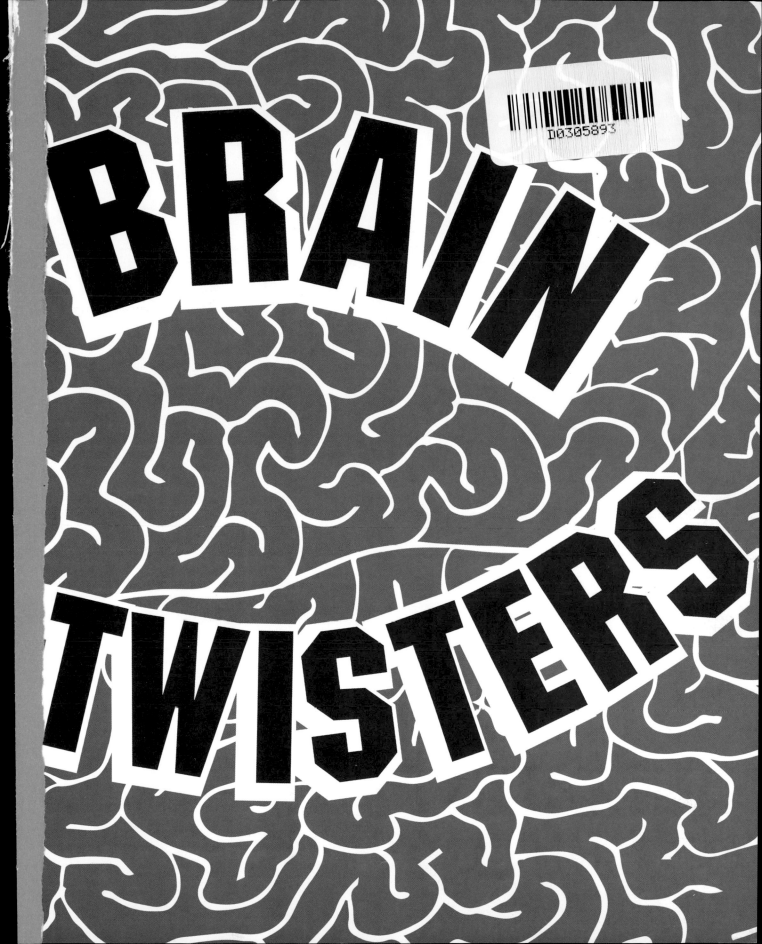

BRAIN TWISTERS

BRAIN TWISTERS

CLIVE GIFFORD

Consultant **Professor Anil Seth**

IVY KIDS

First published in the UK in 2015 by

Ivy Press

210 High Street

Lewes

East Sussex BN7 2NS

United Kingdom

www.ivypress.co.uk

ISBN: 978-1-78240-204-6

This book was conceived, designed & produced by

Ivy Press

CREATIVE DIRECTOR	Peter Bridgewater
COMMISSIONING EDITOR	Georgia Amson-Bradshaw
MANAGING EDITOR	Hazel Songhurst
PROJECT EDITOR	Polly Goodman
CONSULTANT	Professor Anil Seth
ART DIRECTOR	Kim Hankinson
DESIGNER	Ginny Zeal

Printed in China

Origination by Ivy Press Reprographics

1 3 5 7 9 10 8 6 4 2

Distributed worldwide (except North America)
by Thames & Hudson Ltd,
181A High Holborn, London WC1V 7QX, United Kingdom

CONTENTS

YOUR AMAZING BRAIN

You are amazing. You've already proven it by opening this book and reading these words! Reading is just one of hundreds of tasks you do every day; one of many decisions you make and actions you perform. At the centre of it all is your truly amazing brain. It not only keeps you alive by helping to regulate all your body's functions, it also allows you to learn, solve problems, remember and perform. In short, your brain is your nanny, security guard, advisor and secretary all rolled up into one.

But before you get smug, you need to know that you and your brain aren't 100 percent perfect. Your brain doesn't always make sense of your senses, doesn't always understand or perform as you would like it to, and doesn't always remember and recall everything with perfect precision. This book is all about the ways your brain works and changes over time. It looks at some twists, tricks and activities you can perform to demonstrate your brain's powers, and shows how your brain solves problems and influences your emotions and personality. So, get your brain working and dive in!

Here's a taster of just some of the things you'll find out in this book.

SCARED STIFF

Scared of spiders? Turn to page 50 to learn about the part of your brain that triggers your fear mechanism, and to find out how the brain judges risk and, sometimes, gets it wrong.

SEEING IN 3D

Your eyes may be spaced apart to give you depth of vision but it is your amazing brain and its processing power that gives you much of your ability to see and manipulate shapes and space in three dimensions. Turn to page 39 to learn more.

PLAYING TRICKS

Your eyes and brain combine to give you an astonishingly good vision system, but it can make mistakes or be tricked by optical illusions as you'll find on pages 22–23.

THE PHYSICAL BRAIN

One and a half kilos of pinky-beige wobbly jelly may not sound like much to shout about, but this mass of material is home to some of the most remarkable work performed on Earth. Human brains have been responsible for breath-taking discoveries, inventions and works of art, but what is even more astonishing is the vast amount of ordinary work each person's brain gets through every single day.

Your brain is a rapid response data-processing hub.

INFORMATION HIGHWAY

Your brain handles thousands of 'shout outs' from all parts of your body every hour. These signals tell the brain about the condition and position of each body part. All this data travels through your network of nerves and must be filtered, sorted and, in some cases, acted upon by your brain.

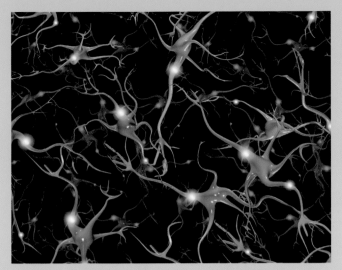

MUSCLE MASTER

The brain sends vast numbers of instructions to your body's muscles every day. These travel through the nervous system and order muscles to contract (get shorter) or relax (get longer). Each movement you make, from sitting down to making a fencing lunge, involves many muscles all working together – your brain has to coordinate all their movements with perfect precision.

NETWORK OF NEURONS

Your brain is packed with millions of nerve cells known as neurons. Each brain neuron creates links with lots of others to form an incredible neural network. These connections aren't fixed, they can alter and new ones form. Scientists estimate more than one million new connections are made in your brain every day.

ALL SORTS OF THOUGHTS

Beliefs about the brain have changed greatly. The Ancient Greeks, for example, thought the brain maintained body temperature, while the heart regulated intelligence. Since then, many scientists have discovered much about how the brain really works, and the varied jobs it performs.

THE NAKED BRAIN

The human brain is protected inside a bony crash helmet, better known as the skull, and by thin layers of material between the skull and brain called membranes or meninges. Between two layers of membrane lies cerebrospinal fluid. This surrounds the brain and acts as a shock absorber. It, along with a network of arteries (blood vessels carrying blood from the heart), bring oxygen, energy and nutrients to the brain.

Your brain is divided up into a number of parts. The outer part is the largest. It's called the cerebral cortex, or cerebrum, and is split into right and left halves, known as hemispheres. Each hemisphere is divided by scientists into four sections called lobes. These are each believed to be responsible for a range of different tasks. The brain is connected to your spinal cord (see page 12) by the brain stem, and behind the brain stem is the cerebellum, which helps organize all the signals sent to your body's muscles.

FRONTAL LOBE

Geniuses take note: this is where your serious, deeper thinking is mostly performed. The frontal lobes are responsible for problem solving, planning and pondering. They also control most of the voluntary body movements you make.

Side view

TEMPORAL LOBE

Responsible for listening and understanding sound, these lobes are also involved in your speech, memory and emotion.

PARIETAL LOBE

Much information from your senses, such as taste, touch, pain and temperature, is processed here. The parietal lobes help decide the order in which all the information is dealt with.

THALAMUS

This busy brain part relays information from your senses to other parts of your brain, helps control your movement and also regulates your cycle of sleeping and waking.

OCCIPITAL LOBE

These large lobes process signals sent from your eyes via the optic nerve to give you vision.

Cross-section

View from above

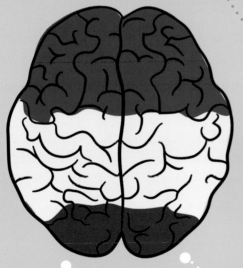

CEREBELLUM

This second, 'little brain' at the rear of your brain coordinates your muscles and movement, and helps you keep your balance and understand distances to and from objects. The cerebellum has more neurons than the entire rest of the brain.

LEFT AND RIGHT HEMISPHERES

The two halves of the cerebral cortex are heavily folded on their surfaces. They are joined to each other by many millions of nerve cells.

BRAIN STEM

This connects your brain to your spinal cord (see page 12). It's also responsible for many of your most basic life functions such as controlling heartbeat, blood pressure and breathing.

GETTING ON YOUR NERVES

Did you know that inside your body lies the world's single most complex object? Your nervous system is made up of vast numbers of nerve cells (neurons) — nearly 90 thousand million of them! Each nerve cell is connected to many others and the total number of connections is truly astronomical.

The brain is just one part of your nervous system. It also includes large bundles of nerve fibres made of nerve cells, which connect the brain to the body. Signals pass along these bundles in both directions, so your brain can control both what is going on inside your body as well as the actions it takes on the outside.

NERVOUS NETWORK

Your nervous system is made up of two regions: central and peripheral. The central nervous system is made up of the spinal cord and the brain, and is connected to the peripheral nervous system by a collection of 43 different pairs of nerves.

Thousands of peripheral nerves stretch out through all parts of your body, carrying tiny electric signals to and from the central nervous system. The central nervous system is an information superhighway, buzzing with activity as it channels all the signals sent to and from the brain.

The central nervous system runs inside your spinal cord up to your brain.

The median nerve runs the length of your arm, from your fingertips to the shoulder. It is a major peripheral nerve that sends and receives signals from the central nervous system.

A NEURON UP CLOSE

A neuron collects signals from other neurons through its finger-like projections, called dendrites. The signal then passes through the neuron as an electrical pulse, but special chemicals, called neurotransmitters, are required for the next step. These help the signal leave the axon — the long, thread-like part of the neuron — and jump to the dendrites of the next neuron, where it continues its journey. Each neuron may be connected to one, two or even thousands of other neurons through its branching mesh of dendrites and axons.

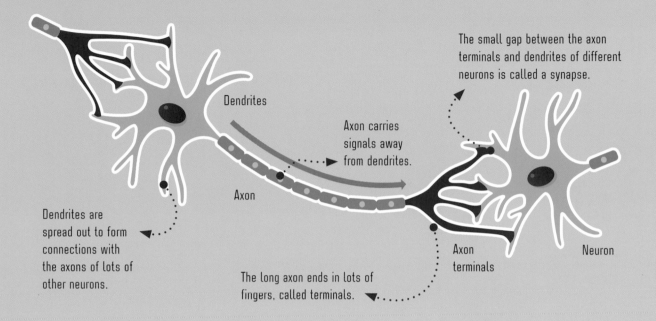

The small gap between the axon terminals and dendrites of different neurons is called a synapse.

Dendrites

Axon carries signals away from dendrites.

Axon

Dendrites are spread out to form connections with the axons of lots of other neurons.

The long axon ends in lots of fingers, called terminals.

Axon terminals

Neuron

TEST YOUR REACTIONS

Your nervous system is no slouch. Signals conveyed by neurons can race through your body at high speed, up to 480 kilometres per hour — faster than a Formula 1 car! To see these speedy signals in action, perform a reaction test using a long ruler.

Ask someone to hold the top of the ruler with the other end just in line with your thumb and index finger, which should be open and not touching the ruler. Without warning, they should release the ruler and you must catch it between your thumb and finger as quickly as you can.

Perform the experiment five times, noting where on the ruler your finger and thumb grip. Add the five measurements together, then divide by five to get your average reaction distance. Use the following handy table to rate your reactions.

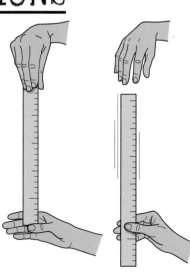

EXCELLENT	ABOVE AVERAGE	AVERAGE	BELOW AVERAGE	POOR
<7.5cm	7.5–15.9cm	16–20.4cm	20.5–28cm	>28cm

A BRAIN OF TWO HALVES

Meet your two-sided brain. It's divided into two halves, or hemispheres — a right and a left. The two sides of the brain are connected by a thick band of nerve fibres, called the corpus callosum, which contains an estimated 200–250 million neurons.

Each side of your brain may have some specialisms. The left hemisphere, for example, is thought to be more heavily involved in certain aspects of understanding language. However in the majority of tasks, the two halves of the brain mostly work together.

Right side

Left side

The left side of the brain controls the right arm and leg.

The right side of the brain controls the left arm and leg.

SWITCHING

The right hemisphere of your brain controls the left side of your body, while the left hemisphere controls the right side. When you touch something with your right hand, nerve signals relating to touch travel up to the left side of your brain. The same is the case with the motor signals that your brain sends out to control your muscles and movement of your body. So, when you wave your left hand to say hello or try to score a goal with a left-footed shot, it's the right side of your brain doing the instructing.

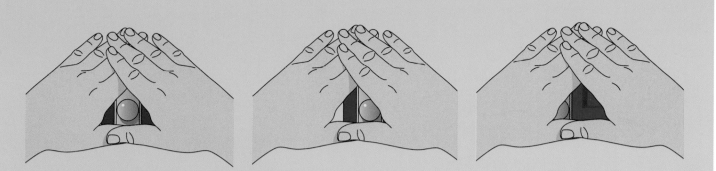

YOUR DOMINANT EYE

You may have heard of being left- or right-handed, but did you know you may also have a dominant eye? Hold your hands as in the picture, creating a small, triangular gap or viewfinder a couple of centimetres wide. Focus on something that fills the gap 5 metres or more away, for example part of a door. Keeping your head and hands still, close one eye and keep focusing on the object. Then switch eyes. Whichever open eye keeps the object most within your viewfinder is your dominant eye.

Is he smiling or grimacing?

HAPPY OR SAD?

Having a dominant left or right field of vision can mean that your brain pays more attention to one side of an image, or overrides the information on the other, less dominant side. Stare at the tip of the nose of the person in the picture (right) for five seconds, then look away. Answer the question: did the person seem more happy or more sad? Most people's (around 70 percent) dominant field of vision is their left side (the side with the smile), so 'happy' is the more likely conclusion.

DELVING DEEPER

Deep in the core of your brain lie fundamental brain structures, which scientists believe reach back deep into our evolutionary past. Together, they form the limbic system and they perform an extremely wide range of different tasks.

One part of the limbic system, the hippocampus, helps pick which information is passed on to long-term memory and is involved with learning. Other parts of the limbic system help generate your emotions, keep you alert and keep many of your body systems running smoothly.

LIMBIC SYSTEM

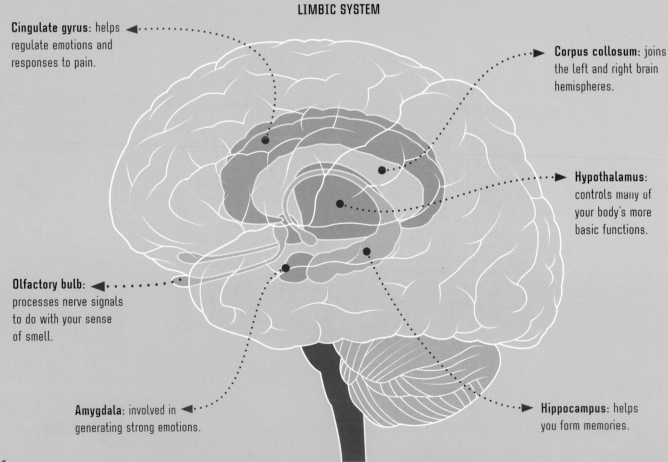

Cingulate gyrus: helps regulate emotions and responses to pain.

Corpus collosum: joins the left and right brain hemispheres.

Hypothalamus: controls many of your body's more basic functions.

Olfactory bulb: processes nerve signals to do with your sense of smell.

Amygdala: involved in generating strong emotions.

Hippocampus: helps you form memories.

KEEPING YOU TICKING OVER

The hypothalamus is only about the size of an almond and weighs just 4 grams. For such a tiny size it sure works hard, helping your body perform many tasks without actively thinking about them. The hypothalamus is a key link between your nervous system and endocrine system. It sends out chemical messengers called hormones, which affect different body parts. Some hormones, for example, help prompt smooth muscle contractions to move food through your digestive system. Others help adjust your internal body temperature, appetite, blood pressure, and many more things besides.

The hypothalamus receives lots of information from nerves about the condition of the body and its parts. In response, it either releases some hormones directly or prompts its neighbour, the pituitary gland, to release the hormones.

TEST YOUR REFLEXES

Some actions occur without your brain being involved, such as blinking when entering bright sunlight. These actions are known as reflexes, and they involve signals travelling to and from the spinal cord without reaching the brain, along a simple pathway called a reflex arc.

To see one reflex in action, get someone to sit down and cross their legs so that their top leg can swing freely. Use the side of your hand to tap the top leg just below the kneecap. If you tap the right place, the person's leg will kick forward involuntarily, all in just 0.05 seconds!

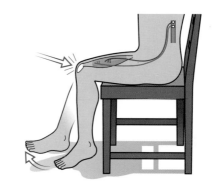

GETTING ALL EMOTIONAL

Parts of the limbic system are believed to play important roles in generating your emotions, including sadness and crying. The amygdala, for instance, is involved in producing the strong emotions of fear and anger connected with survival, including your fight or flight response to danger (see pages 50–51), whilst the cingulate gyrus may regulate emotional responses, especially to pain. Scientists have also found that parts of the hypothalamus may be responsible for generating loud, uncontrollable laughter.

THE BUSY BRAIN

Even when you're doing nothing and just chilling out, your brain has the accelerator pushed hard to the floor. It's always at work, even when you don't think it is, never fully rests and remains active on a 24/7 basis. It's so busy that it uses over 20 percent of all the oxygen your body takes in from the air.

Your brain also consumes around 20 percent of all the glucose sugar your digestive system generates from your food as fuel to power its activity. Both oxygen and glucose, as well as other nutrients, are carried to your brain by a system of blood vessels. As much as a litre of blood can flow through these vessels every minute.

Seeing: using your sense of sight activates the occipital lobes at the back of the brain.

Listening: the auditory area of the temporal lobes become active when hearing.

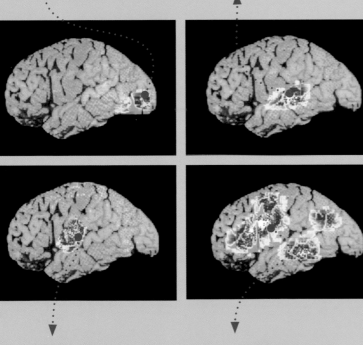

THE 10 PERCENT MYTH

Some people still believe an old myth that we use only 10 percent of our brain. They're wrong! Science has shown that we use virtually every part of our brain at different times depending on the tasks the brain needs to perform. Positron Emission Tomography (PET) scans (left) can show, for instance, how different areas of the brain are activated by different tasks. The more active part of the brain in each example is shown in red and yellow. In the bottom right image, thinking about grammar and language whilst speaking creates an explosion of activity in many parts of the brain.

Speaking: speaking produces activity in the speech centres in the insula and motor cortex parts of the brain.

Thinking about language and speaking: lots of parts of the brain become more active.

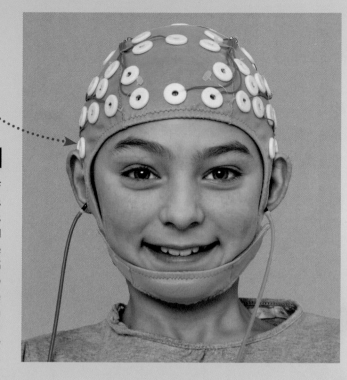

There's electricity inside this cap!

BRIGHT SPARKS

Your brain is a constant, seething mass of electrical and chemical activity as neurons fire to transmit signals through its various parts. Different types of medical scans and tests can measure the energy used or the electricity generated by your neurons. An EEG (electroencephalogram), for example, uses a cap covered in small electrodes to detect and measure electrical patterns of brain activity. Each time a neuron fires, it generates a tiny amount of electricity. When lots of neurons fire, they can be detected and measured by the electrodes.

KEEP A SLEEP AND DREAM DIARY

Your brain remains active even when you're asleep. Your sleep comes in different stages. You tend to dream during the Rapid Eye Movement (REM) stage.

Keep a record of how you sleep and dream in a journal or notebook for a month. Keep it close to your bed so that you can write down your dreams as soon as you wake up. Record the times you went to bed and awoke, whether you slept well or woke a lot during the night, and as much detail about your dreams as possible, including how they made you feel.

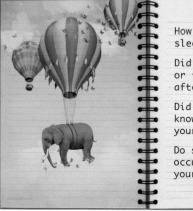

How many hours sleep did you get?

Did you feel tired or full of energy after each sleep?

Did anyone you know appear in your dreams?

Do similar themes occur in many of your dreams?

MAKING SENSE

2

Trapped inside your skull, your brain cannot directly experience the rest of you or your surroundings. So it relies on information from other parts of your body to work out what you're doing, and what's happening around you. Much of this information is generated by your senses.

You may have been taught that you have five senses: sight, hearing, touch, taste and smell. In fact, the truth is that you have a number of senses beyond those. Here are some of them.

OUCH!

Your body's pain receptors send signals to your brain via your nervous system. Your sense of pain acts as a warning system, stopping you from doing something that is causing damage to your body.

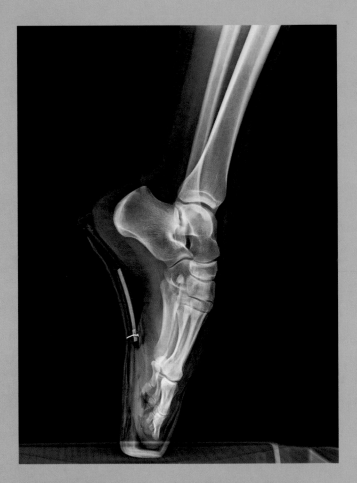

BALANCING THINGS OUT

Your brain, inner ear and other parts of your body form the vestibular system, which allows you to stay steady and upright when moving or performing challenging balances.

BRRRRR!

The layers of your skin contain a number of thermoreceptors — special nerve cells that respond when hot or cold. Together, they can help determine the temperature of an object and your surroundings.

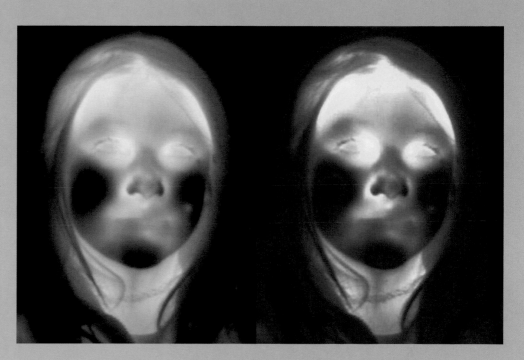

Have you ever wondered how you touch your nose with your eyes closed?

NICE CATCH!

Proprioception is a sense that tells your brain the location of all the parts of your body. It often works with your sense of sight to aid coordinated activities like catching a ball or making movements with your eyes closed.

HUNGER PANGS

Your sense of hunger is prompted by the release of hormones in your body. When your stomach is empty, a hormone called ghrelin is released, stimulating your appetite.

21

SEEING STRAIGHT

Shaped like bulging balls and filled with a clear jelly, your eyes gather in vast amounts of information about the visual world. Light reflected from an object travels through the transparent cornea and the pupil (the black hole at the front of your eye). It is then refracted (bent) by the curved, see-through lens and focused on the retina at the back of the eye.

The retina is packed with millions of photoreceptor cells, which react to different wavelengths of light. The cells change light signals into electrical signals, which travel along your optic nerve to your brain, where the image is processed. A single optic nerve is made up of around one million nerve fibres.

An upside-down image forms on the retina. Don't worry, the brain turns things the right way up!

Light rays reflected from an object enter the eye through the pupil.

Optic nerve

The lens bends the light rays as they pass through.

YOUR BLIND SPOT

Hold this book at arm's length, close your left eye and focus on the girl. As you slowly bring the book towards you, the ball should disappear, then reappear. This is due to your blind spot, an area where the optic nerve joins the retina, which lacks photoreceptor cells.

OPTICAL ILLUSIONS

Your eyes and sense of sight are amazing, but they are not perfect and can be fooled by optical illusions. Some illusions use images which your eyes and brain struggle to compare for size, colour or how far away objects in the image appear. Other illusions exploit how your eyes constantly scan the view in front of them, by creating a still image that appears to move in front of you. Stare closely at this pattern and you'll find the circles start to pulse outwards before your eyes.

ARE TWO EYES BETTER THAN ONE?

When you look at something, each eye sees a slightly different view. These signals are merged in the brain to give you good depth perception – knowledge of how far away an object is. To test this out, place a cup 30–40 centimetres away and close one eye. Ask someone to hold a small ball around 30–50 centimetres above the cup and move it around. Shout, 'Drop!' when you want the ball released into the cup. Do this six times with the cup placed in different positions, then attempt it six times with both eyes open. You should see your score soar!

SISTER SENSES

Your incredible nose, working with your brain, can tell the difference between approximately 10,000 smells — from a particular brand of perfume to the unmistakeable stench of your sweaty sports socks. Air breathed in through the nostrils contains odour molecules. They are detected by smell receptor cells in the olfactory bulbs, which lie in the roof of the nasal cavity.

Your sense of taste comes courtesy of around 10,000 taste buds. These are found on the roof and sides of your mouth, and on your tongue. Your taste buds can detect five basic tastes: sour, bitter, sweet, salty and umami (a savoury taste found in meats, cheeses and mushrooms).

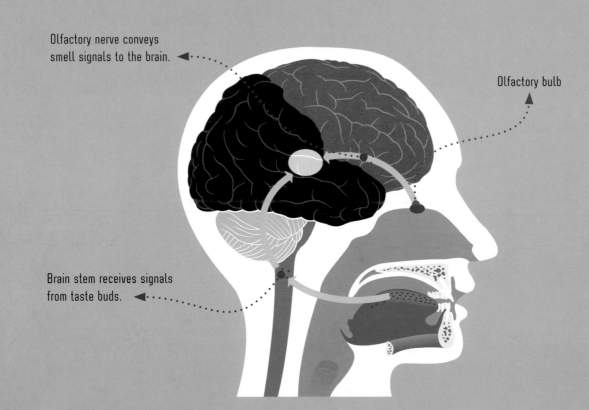

Olfactory nerve conveys smell signals to the brain. ◄

Olfactory bulb

Brain stem receives signals from taste buds. ◄

PATH TO THE BRAIN

Your olfactory bulbs are no bigger than a thumbnail, but they do all your smelling for you. Their many millions of receptor cells each have fine, hair-like projections called cilia, which capture odour molecules. These cause neurons to send signals to the olfactory nerve, which carries them to the brain. In a similar way, nerve cells in your taste buds transmit signals, which are carried by three different nerves through your head to the brain stem.

TRICK YOUR TASTE BUDS

Empty a packet of different flavoured sweets into a bowl. Hold your nose, close your eyes, and randomly pick and place one sweet in your mouth. Try to guess its flavour as it dissolves.

After 30 seconds, let go of your nose and guess the flavour again. Repeat several times with different flavoured sweets.

You are far more likely to guess the flavour when you can use your sense of smell to help. Taste can only distinguish between five broad groups of tastes. It is highly dependent on your sense of smell to determine a precise flavour, which is why food tastes dull when you have a heavy cold and cannot smell well.

What do you see?

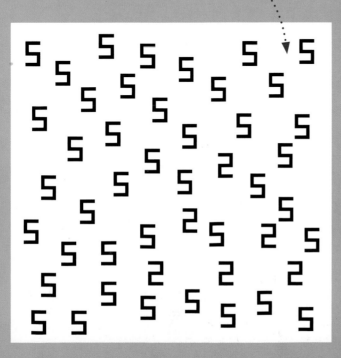

SENSES MERGER

The use of smell and taste to determine a food flavour shows two senses working together. Some people have a condition called synaesthesia, which causes their senses to mingle so they may experience colours, tastes or smells when they read words, view numbers or hear certain sounds. Stare at this picture devised by neuroscientists Vilayanur Ramachandran and Edward Hubbard for five seconds, then look away. What did you see? The answer is lots of the number 5, but also six number 2s. What shape did they form? Many people with synaesthesia would see 2s in a different colour from 5s and so spot the triangle shape made by the 2s, with ease.

TOUCHY FEELY

Your sense of touch is a lot like many senses rolled up into one. There are lots of different types of touch receptors in your body, many found in the layers of your skin, which all sense different stimuli such as pressure, light and heavy touches, and vibrations.

These sensors send back signals through the nervous system up through your spinal cord, brain stem and thalamus to your somatosensory cortex in your brain. Your sense of touch is able to determine textures and shapes, allowing your brain to identify many objects with your eyes closed.

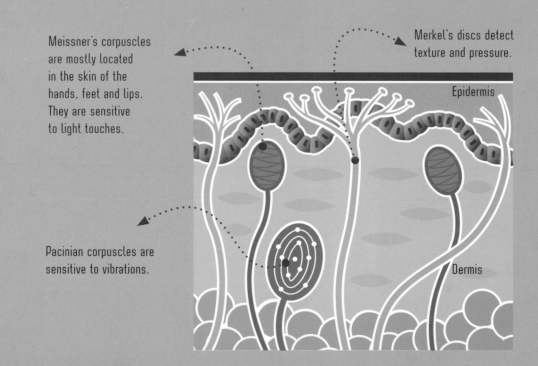

Meissner's corpuscles are mostly located in the skin of the hands, feet and lips. They are sensitive to light touches.

Merkel's discs detect texture and pressure.

Epidermis

Pacinian corpuscles are sensitive to vibrations.

Dermis

SKIN SENSORS

Your skin, all 4 kilograms or so of it, is the largest sense organ in your body. It consists of an outer layer called the epidermis, which covers the dermis, and below that a fatty layer of subcutaneous tissue. Your skin is packed with different sensors (above) that can each play their part in your overall experience of touch, such as when you touch a sharp pin point or wrap a icepack on an injured body part.

TOUCH TEST

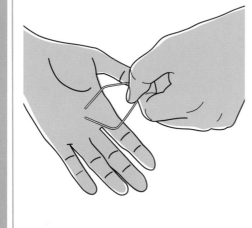

Different parts of your body have a greater or lesser concentration of touch receptors, which give you more or less sensitivity. Find out where the highest concentrations of touch receptors lie using this Two-point Discrimination test.

Bend a paper clip into an open U-shape so that its tips are 2 centimetres apart. Close your eyes or look away as you touch different parts of your body (fingertips, cheek, palm and stomach, for example). Note down where you feel two separate points and where only one. Re-bend the paperclip to 1 centimetre width and re-test the areas where you felt two points. You can also bend the paperclip wider than 2 centimetres and re-test where you only felt one point. The smaller the distance where you can still feel two points, the greater the concentration of touch receptors.

Touch the sides of both fingers at the same time. Does it feel like one pen or two?

TRICKING YOUR TOUCH

Tricking your sense of touch is as easy as crossing your middle and ring fingers and grabbing a pen. Looking away, try to touch the small V shape formed by your crossed fingers with the pen. There's every chance you will feel as if you are being touched by two different pens. This is known as the Aristotle Illusion and is due to the sides of the fingers touching the pen normally being well apart from each other, making the brain conclude that you are touching two objects.

EAR, HEAR

Sound travels as vibrating waves of pressure. Your ears are capable of gathering in both loud and quiet sounds, amplifying them (making them louder) and converting them into electrical signals, which your brain processes to give you the sense of hearing.

Your ears are extraordinary objects. They play a major part in the vestibular system, which gives you your sense of balance. Your ears contain the smallest bones found in your body, the ossicles. The smallest of the ossicles, the stapes or stirrup, measures just 3 millimetres by 2.5 millimetres and weighs around 4 milligrams — 0.16 of the weight of a grain of rice.

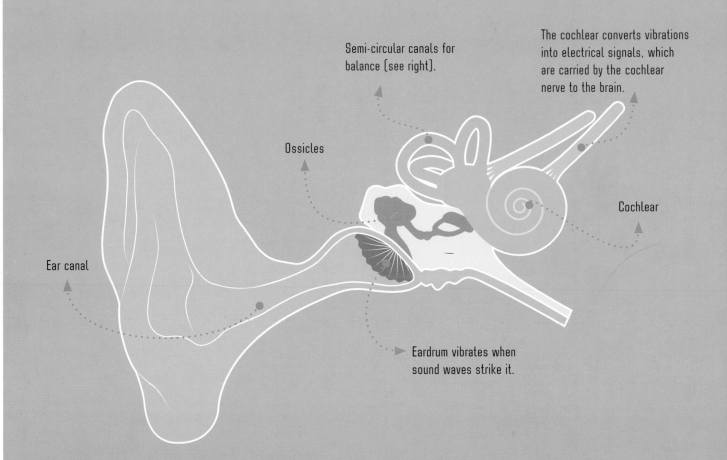

Semi-circular canals for balance (see right).

The cochlear converts vibrations into electrical signals, which are carried by the cochlear nerve to the brain.

Ossicles

Cochlear

Ear canal

Eardrum vibrates when sound waves strike it.

GOOD VIBRATIONS

The outer parts of your ears funnel sound vibrations through a tube called the ear canal into the parts of your ears that are inside your skull. There, the sound waves cause the tympanic membrane (commonly known as the eardrum) to vibrate. The ossicles increase the intensity of these vibrations before they pass through to the cochlear – a coiled tube full of fluid. The cochlear converts the physical movement of the vibrations into electrical signals, which are carried by the cochlear nerve to your brain.

Can you keep your balance?

PROPRIOCEPTION

You can touch parts of your body without looking thanks to your sense of proprioception. This involves proprioceptor cells found in your muscles and joints, which with the help of the brain, give you a sense of where all your body parts are. Test it out by closing your eyes, stretching your arms up and touching your nose and then your right thumb with your left index finger. Repeat and see if your accuracy improves.

KEEPING YOUR BALANCE

A major part of your sense of balance is determined by three semi-circular canals in each ear, which are filled with fluid. Tiny hairs within the canals translate movement of the liquid into electrical messages, which are sent to your brain. You can scramble your sense of balance for a short while by spinning round 5–8 times and then trying to walk along a narrow line without stepping off it. You will find it tricky and may feel a little dizzy. This is because the fluid in the semi-circular canals inside your ears is still sloshing around after you've stopped spinning, confusing your brain.

THINKING ABOUT THINKING

The 90 billion or so neurons in your brain have to manage a phenomenal amount of information sent to them by the body. They also allow you to think in different ways, from reviewing the past to making future plans. In the process of thinking, your brain may filter out irrelevant information and make shortcuts, judgements and assumptions.

Thinking about thinking is called metacognition and can be vital to decision making, as you review all the options as well as check your knowledge and the reliability of your memory. Thinking also helps you figure out multiple problems every day.

MIND YOUR LANGUAGE

Your brain gives you the capacity to express yourself using language and to understand others. Language gives you the ability to think, speak and write, using words as symbols to describe complex ideas.

SOLVING PROBLEMS

Thinking allows you to solve a vast range of different problems, from tricky maths questions to brain-teasers and puzzles, as well as the problems that you encounter in everyday life.

DEEP IN THOUGHT

Sometimes, you may be required to consciously think hard, such as when figuring out a complex problem. Much of the time, though, you are thinking in the background – your brain multitasks, allowing you to think while performing a completely different activity.

SPATIAL AWARENESS

Your brain gives you the ability to think in three dimensions – to visualize and navigate your way through the space that surrounds you. This is known as spatial awareness and is vital when manipulating objects, finding your way or playing most sports.

atten-TION!

Your brain is being bombarded with vast amounts of data from all your senses, such as multiple conversations at school lunchtime, or a mass of visual data ahead of you in a busy street. At the same time, you may be thinking about all sorts of things, from deciding who to invite to your birthday party to recalling something you read earlier. It all adds up to a bewildering amount of information and your brain, amazing as it is, cannot cope with absolutely everything.

So, your brain filters information, weeding out data it thinks doesn't concern or interest you (such as an unexciting conversation between strangers). Instead it tries to focus on information that may be important, such as a sudden movement ahead, or a focused task like seeking out that school jumper you've been searching for in your chaotic bedroom.

RED	BLUE	YELLOW	GREEN	PURPLE
PURPLE	BLUE	RED	YELLOW	BLUE
RED	YELLOW	GREEN	RED	GREEN
GREEN	YELLOW	RED	BLUE	PURPLE
GREEN	YELLOW	PURPLE	PURPLE	BLUE

INTERFERENCE AND THE STROOP EFFECT

Attention can be interfered with, as American psychologist John Ridley Stroop discovered and detailed in 1935, in what has become known as the Stroop Effect. Run through the list of words above as fast as you can, saying the colour that each word is printed in NOT the actual words. Time yourself and then run through the list again, this time reading the actual words.

You should find that your second run is faster than the first, because the words themselves interfere with your ability to say the correct colour quickly. This may be due to how naming the colour of things requires more of your brain's attention than simply reading words out loud.

COMPETING FOR YOUR ATTENTION

Data passes into your short-term sensory memory and is held there for a very short time. Unless your brain focuses attention on this data, it will be erased and lost. Take a look at the picture above and try to find the six objects listed below:

- cherry
- zebra
- safety pin
- button
- music box key
- seahorse

With your attention being focused on this one task, you should find them relatively quickly.

Now go and do something else for a short while, then return to the image. Look for the same six objects below whilst saying out loud all the things you have eaten in the last 24 hours. Chances are that you will find each object more slowly because your attention is being divided between two different tasks.

Find me!

MAGIC
MISDIRECTION

Are you paying attention? You may think so, but your brain can be distracted or channelled into focusing on one thing at the expense of another. Magicians often exploit and make use of this in order to keep your attention away from something else — a technique called misdirection.

This technique uses a big gesture or flourish that your brain focuses on in order to distract your attention away from another movement or object, which is a key part of a magician's trick.

BLIND TO CHANGE

Change blindness is the tendency of the brain not to spot a change in a visual stimulus because of distractions to its attention. Look at the image (above left) of basketball players for a few seconds and then stare at the image next to it. The second image has blots of grey over it. These distract attention and make it harder for you to spot a significant difference between the two photos. Can you see it? See page 63 for the answer.

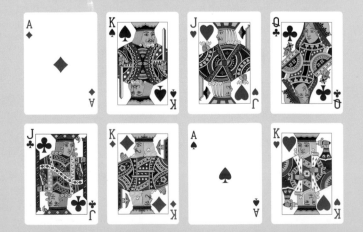

34

FAKE BALL TOSS

Magicians sometimes rely on people's brains expecting objects to move or behave in a certain, familiar way. They can misdirect their audience with a simple fake ball toss. Using a sponge ball, the magician throws it straight up a couple of times. As he goes to toss the ball again, he grips the ball with his fingers but makes the regular throwing movement upwards and moves his head as if watching the flight of the ball. The audience's brain predicts what it expects to happen based on what it has seen before and also follows the expected ball's path, only to be befuddled when the ball seemingly disappears.

Ball shown in hand before being thrown upwards.

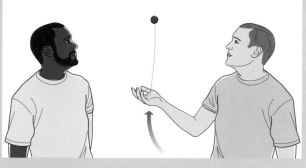

Magician and audience's head follows the ball's flight.

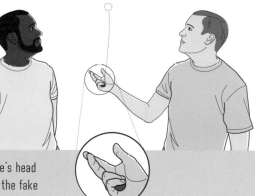

Audience's head follows the fake throw expecting a real ball.

Try this simple trick on your friends.

HUNT THE CARD

Look hard at the eight cards on the left and pick one. Turn away from the page for a count of 20, remembering your card, then search for your card in the seven cards on the right. Can you find it? Your card has disappeared! What you may not have spotted straight away though is that all of the eight cards have been replaced by other cards – you were too focused on your card to notice the changes to the others.

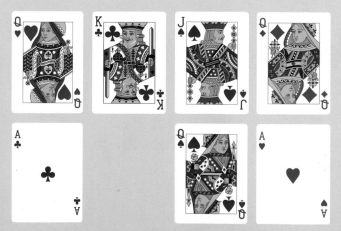

GUESSING GAMES

Stuck in your skull, your brain relies on your senses and the vast amount of data they produce. It frequently has to make best guesses rather than be absolutely certain. To do this, it relies on its ability to recognize, remember and use patterns to speed up its processing.

Some of these shortcuts are in your perception — interpreting all the data your senses generate. Others are cognitive — your brain makes best guesses or assumptions from memory to fill in gaps in the information it possesses.

FILLING IN THE GAPS

Look at the pair of images on the right Can you see two big white triangles? How many triangles can you count in total? The surprising answer is there are no actual triangles in the image. What's happening is that when objects are grouped together, your brain tends to see them as a whole, ignoring gaps and mentally adding lines or edges to turn the image into something that is more familiar. These are called subjective contours and this illusion is known as the Kanizsa Triangle illusion after Italian psychologist Gaetano Kanizsa, who first described it in 1955.

SEEKING OUT PATTERNS

Your brain makes use of remembered data and patterns in memory to find matches or identify things when it encounters something new or unfamiliar. Take a good look at the image above. At first glance it just looks like a random collection of black splodges, but look longer and your brain may begin assembling a pattern familiar to it from memory on the right-hand side of the image. Can you see what it is? See page 63 for the answer.

Be patient and keep looking... your brain should eventually recognize a pattern.

GETTING IT WRONG

Two plumbers are fixing a leaking sink. Plumber A is plumber B's son, but plumber B is not plumber A's father. Does this statement puzzle you? This is because your brain likes to label things and seek out familiar patterns which it believes are true because they have worked for you in the past.

This can lead to assumptions such as certain jobs only being performed by men, like professional boxers... or plumbers. Take away the assumption that the plumbers in the picture are male and the answer becomes clear – plumber B is a woman and plumber A's mother.

Plumber A   Plumber B

INTELLIGENT LIFE

Intelligence comes in a wide range of forms, including verbal intelligence (the ability to understand and use language), musical intelligence (the ability to recognize and pick up pitch, tone and rhythm) and bodily-kinesthetic intelligence (the ability to manipulate objects, coordinate body movements and use a wide range of physical skills).

People with logical-mathematical intelligence, for example, may be excellent at calculating sums and solving equations as well as having strong logic skills (see pages 40–41).

MULTIPLE INTELLIGENCE

This busker not only exhibits musical intelligence to play his instrument well, he also displays verbal and spatial intelligence to figure out and communicate directions to a passer-by. When he works out how much money he has made, he will demonstrate logical-mathematical intelligence.

VERBAL INTELLIGENCE

Having good verbal-linguistic intelligence tends to mean that you can read quickly, take in information easily and express yourself well in speech and writing. Sometimes, it means being able to learn foreign languages easily. One element of verbal intelligence is being able to learn and recall a wide vocabulary of words, so try this simple verbal intelligence test. How many words (not including proper nouns) can you make out of the letters in the word 'verbally'? If you can get more than 10, you're doing well. Over 20 and you're a champion!

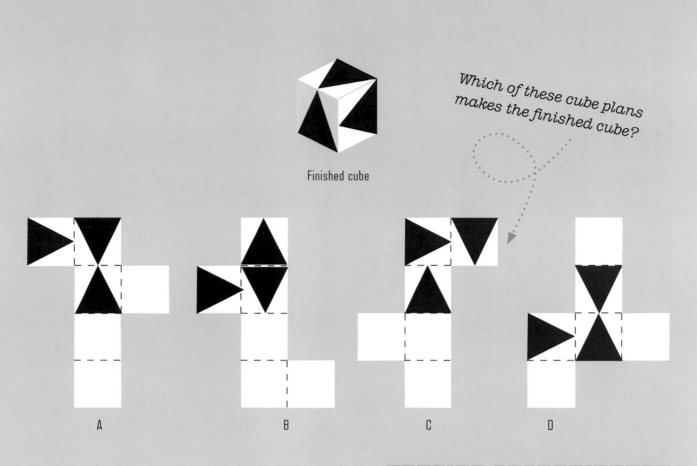

Finished cube

Which of these cube plans makes the finished cube?

A   B   C   D

SPATIAL INTELLIGENCE

Your ability to think in shapes, space and in three dimensions is known as your spatial awareness or spatial intelligence. If you have high levels of spatial intelligence, you may be good at finding your way through mazes or solving visual puzzles, understanding machines and how they work, and reading maps. You can test out your spatial intelligence with these two tests. First, try to figure out which of the four flat patterns could be folded to make the cube. Then see if you can work out which of the four sets of shapes can be rearranged to form the parallelogram. See page 63 for the answers.

Which set of shapes can form the finished parallelogram?

Finished parallelogram

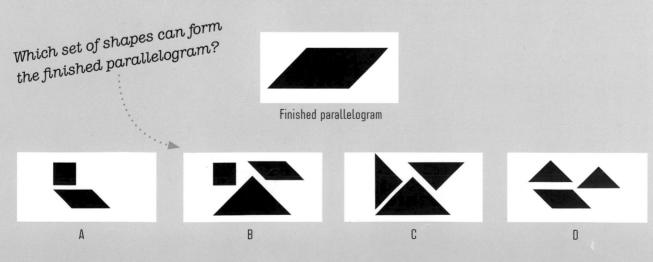

A   B   C   D

LOGICAL THINKING

Logic is about understanding how pieces of information relate to each other, thinking clearly, and using reasoning to figure out an accurate answer or conclusion from known facts. The building blocks of a logical argument are statements or facts known as propositions.

Propositions are examined to find out whether they're true or false. Using a number of true propositions linked together, you can deduce a conclusion. For example, the two propositions, 'All mammals have lungs' and 'A whale is a mammal' can lead you to the conclusion that all whales have lungs.

DECISIONS AND DEDUCTIONS

You use logic in order to make decisions every day. The flow chart below shows a short chain of logical statements concerned with replacing a broken television. Another piece of logical thinking might see you ask a series of questions to work out the identity of a playing card. Asking whether the card is red or black, a number or picture card, and whether it is female or male might, if the reply to each question is the first answer, lead you to deduce that the card is either the Queen of Hearts or Diamonds.

'I want to buy a new TV.'

'TVs are sold in electrical shops.'

'So, I can go to an electrical shop to buy a TV.'

NUMBERS GAME

Popular number puzzles and games like Sudoku and Kakuro rely more on logic than mathematical skills. All the maths you need to play and solve them is the ability to add numbers correctly. The same is the case with the number puzzler to the left. Can you position the numbers 4, 5, 6, 7, 8 and 9 in the empty circles so that the numbers on each side of the triangle add up to the same total? Find out how it's done on page 63.

1

2   3

Use logical thinking to solve these puzzles.

THINKING OUT OF THE BOX

Logic puzzles are often little stories or problems that can be solved if you think logically about the possible outcomes. Here's one. You visit a fruit stall where there are three boxes. The first is labelled pineapples, the second bananas and the third, pineapples and bananas. All three boxes are labelled wrongly! You may ask the stall owner to pick one item from any one of the boxes, but only one box. With no other information, how can you label the boxes correctly? Find the answer on page 63.

SOLVING PROBLEMS

Your brain is like a well-stocked toolbox, equipped with a range of different tools or techniques. It can use these to solve a range of problems, from cracking a code to finding your way around an unfamiliar town.

Sometimes, logic alone may be enough to overcome a problem, but on other occasions you may need to recall key information from memory, spot connections between two different things, or recognize patterns in the data your brain receives.

TOWERING TEST

Trial and error involves you trying out a number of possible solutions, noting what works and what doesn't, and learning from your mistakes until you complete a solution. Many people use trial and error to tackle the Tower of Hanoi puzzle (below), which is a tough test of people's problem-solving skills. The aim is to move each disc over to the tower on the far right while following three rules:

1. You can only move one disc at a time.
2. Only the top disc on a stack can be moved.
3. No disc can be put on top of a smaller disc.

To see how it's done look online for an animated solution.

Get all the discs on to this tower following the rules.

REASONING RIDDLES

Recalling known facts from memory can be useful in solving some problems, including this riddle, which is in the form of a question: 'During which month do people sleep the least?'

Turn to page 63 for the answer, but only after having a good, long think about what you know.

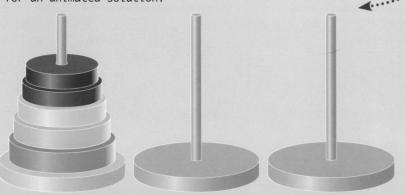

DECISIONS DECISIONS

Other factors besides logic and memory recall can influence the way you solve problems and make decisions. Your emotions often sway your decisions, too. For example, the thrill of a fast-moving auction may see people bid more for an item than they intended. The emotional desire to win the auction and another emotion, fear (of losing out) can prompt this behaviour.

Next time you make a decision, think about how much it was affected by logic and how much by emotion.

SENSIBLE DECISION?

Here's another example of a decision not based on logic. You go to a shop to buy a tablet case. It's priced at £10 but the sale, which starts tomorrow, reduces it to just £2. A week later a tablet is priced at £499 but it will be on sale the next day for £491. In both cases, do you buy the items straight away or return in the sale? If you applied only logic, you would do the same thing both times as the saving is £8 in each case. However, studies show that most people will wait to buy the tablet case at the lower price but wouldn't make an extra trip for the tablet.

FEELING FEELINGS

Every day, you find yourself dealing with feelings, or emotions, from envy at someone's new clothes or guilt about something you haven't done, to surprise and joy at good news or pride in an achievement. Your emotions may be prompted by your surroundings, such as seeing a beautiful view or watching a scary movie, or they may come from your reactions to other people and how they communicate with you.

Emotions are deep, inner feelings, such as fear, disgust, anger and joy, which affect your brain and your body. Your emotions influence how you behave, whether it's fear prompting you to run from danger, or happiness causing you to relax.

How sincere is this smile?

FAKING IT

You may try to hide your real emotions at times, for example, to conceal boredom when visiting a relative or hiding your happiness at a mistake someone has made. People often fake a smile to signal approval, but there are usually tell-tale signs that it isn't genuine from the muscles in the face. Do you think this smile is genuine or fake?

A MATTER OF SURVIVAL

In the past, people relied on their emotions to assess risks and protect themselves from danger in order to survive. Today, you are more likely to use your emotions to plan your life and make ordinary everyday decisions, from who to sit next to in class to what items to buy.

What now?
Follow your feelings...

ALL IN THE MIND

Our understanding of how our emotions work is not yet complete. Scientists do know that a small part of your brain called the amygdala (in yellow, left) is involved in a lot of our emotional responses to things such as threatening sounds and visual information.

LETTING OTHERS KNOW HOW YOU FEEL

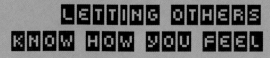

You have a wide range of techniques, from facial expressions and body language to speech (verbal language), with which you can communicate how you feel, your thoughts and your ideas to others. More than one technique is often used at the same time.

GETTING EMOTIONAL

Emotions are complex and powerful inner feelings involving the limbic system, bodily changes and situations you face in life. When you experience an emotion, you tend to experience both a mental 'feeling' such as dread, anger, joy or surprise, but also physical sensations in your body such as your heart beating faster or slower.

Viewing a gory scene may cause you to experience disgust, both as a feeling of revulsion and as a bodily reaction making you want to be physically sick. Emotions seem to prepare both your mind and your body for what happens next. This may be a desire to do something to gain a reward, or an increase in your heart rate and other body systems to ready you for a sudden physical challenge.

MIND AND BODY

If you unexpectedly upset someone, you may 'feel' embarrassed, but your body may react by increasing blood flow to your cheeks, causing you to blush. The varied ways that different parts of the body react to different emotions have been mapped by an innovative study in Finland reported in 2013 (see images below). The areas in red and yellow show an increase in sensations felt in parts of the body and a decrease is shown in the blue or black areas.

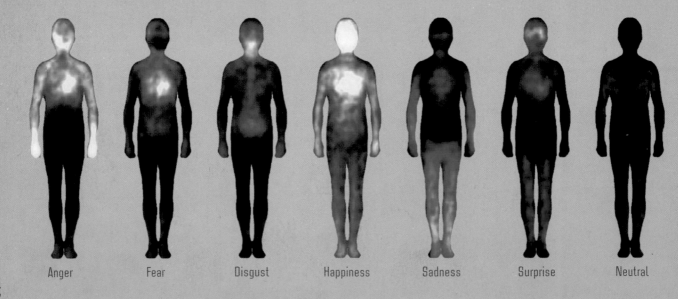

| Anger | Fear | Disgust | Happiness | Sadness | Surprise | Neutral |

ACTING EMOTIONALLY

Scientists remain unsure whether people perceive emotion because the changes to your body come first and are then interpreted by your mind, or whether the body changes come as a result of your brain feeling the emotion. What they do know is that emotions influence your behaviour and many of the decisions you make – a fact understood by advertisers. You may also, at times, be able to feel a faint version of someone else's emotional situation, allowing you to understand how they feel and respond accordingly. This ability is known as empathy.

Can you work out what emotions are being exploited here?

EXPLOITING EMOTIONS

Some advertising appeals to your logic, such as car adverts that state how one model is faster or has better fuel economy than its rivals. Much advertising, though, targets your emotions. This type of advertising might show, for instance, how much fun someone has, or how highly they are rated by others because they bought a product. Some advertising plays on people's insecurities about how they look, such as the before-and-after make-up images on the left, or on emotional fears such as the worry of not fitting in with others.

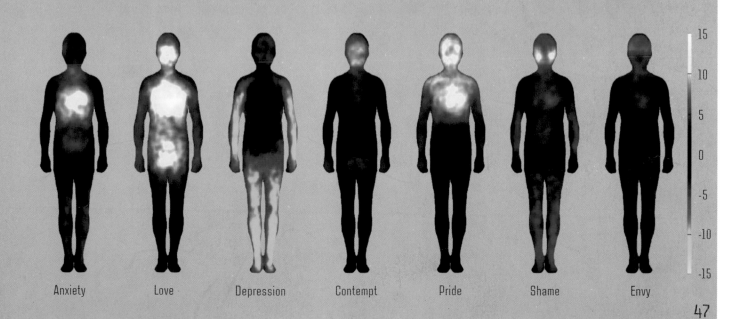

Anxiety   Love   Depression   Contempt   Pride   Shame   Envy

15
10
5
0
-5
-10
-15

SOCIAL ANIMALS

You live, work, learn and play in groups of people who you may depend on for support, survival, education and entertainment. Your brain is equipped to socialize with others and is skilled at understanding verbal language — the meaning of what someone is saying and the way in which they say it.

Your brain is also able to detect other people's feelings without any words being spoken through understanding their non-verbal language. This includes their varying facial expressions, their gestures (such as a happy wave of the hand or a kick of the ground in frustration) and their body language — the different positions a person's body can take.

FACING UP TO FEELINGS

Your face is a picture. With it, you can communicate how you feel, or your reactions to something someone said, and you can 'read' other people's faces to find out how they feel. In 2014, a study mapping the faces of people used computers to describe 21 different facial expressions that all people were able to perform, from awed to happily disgusted. Can you tell what emotions are being displayed in the six photographs of the same person on the right? Chances are, you will get many of these correct. Compare your answers with the ones on page 63.

BODY LANGUAGE

Your body posture and the position and movement of your head, arms and legs can all communicate feelings towards another person, or what they are saying or doing. Leaning towards someone, for example, tends to show that you like them or agree with what they're saying, whilst holding your hands behind your back may send a message that says 'I'm nervous'. Can you guess whether the person furthest right is displaying body language that is defensive, aggressive or passive?

Hands on hips indicates someone feels in control and confident.

What do you think this person's body language is indicating?

Feet together can show someone is feeling more passive or submissive.

Crossing legs towards someone can indicate liking and agreement.

INTERPERSONAL INTELLIGENCE

Your ability to both read others' non-verbal communications and understand their feelings is a sign of your interpersonal intelligence – your 'being good with people' skills. Someone with good interpersonal intelligence is adept at communicating themselves, but is also good at assessing other people's emotions and what is driving them to say or do something. They tend to be good at seeing other people's point of view and may be good at resolving conflicts and disagreements with others in a group.

FEAR, PHOBIAS & RISK

Sensing danger and feeling fear are your body's natural survival tools. If you encounter a dangerous situation, the amygdala deep in your brain triggers your fear mechanism. The front of your brain analyses the threat and your adrenal glands release chemicals into your body including adrenalin.

These give your body a quick boost by raising your heart rate and breathing and increasing the blood supply to your muscles. These actions prepare you for any physical effort ahead, such as escaping quickly or combatting the danger. This is called your fight or flight response.

stroke me!

car
aircraft
water
bees
shark

ASSESSING RISK - WHICH IS MOST DANGEROUS?

While swimming in the sea, what's more likely to kill you: the water or a shark? Your brain tries to analyse and grade the risk of possible dangers to you, but it is not always accurate. For example, fear can distort your judgement of risk by overestimating the risk of something that really frightens you actually happening to you. You can also underplay the very real risk posed by less frightening things and situations. Look at the five images on the left and guess the correct order of risk of causing death, from greatest to least.

AND THE WINNER IS...

The correct order of risk is: car, water (drowning), bees, aircraft, shark. You may be afraid of sharks, but the real risk to you is small. An average of just 4.4 people are killed worldwide each year by sharks, yet around 500 people every year are killed by bees, and 459 people died from plane crashes in 2013. These figures are tiny compared to the tens of thousands of people who drown, and the hundreds of thousands of people who die in car accidents every year. However because catastrophes like plane crashes stick well in your memory, you may perceive flying as quite dangerous as your brain overplays the risk of such an event occurring to you.

PHOBIAS

Phobias are a persistent fear of an object or situation that forces a person to avoid it. Common phobias include fear of spiders, heights and flying. People with phobias may experience physical symptoms such as dizziness and increased heart rate, as well as a strong desire to run away. They may not be prepared to even touch a photo depicting their phobia. So, go on, do you really have a phobia of spiders or are you prepared to touch and stroke the picture on the left?

REMEMBER...

Memory is the ability of your brain to store, retain and recall experiences and information from the past. Memory is everything that you remember, from how to do certain everyday tasks to recognizing people that you encounter. Neuroscientists and psychologists divide memory into a number of different types, such as short-term and long-term memories, and implicit or explicit memories.

An explicit memory is one you have deliberately tried to store and recall, such as your login password to a website. An implicit memory is one that is accessed without thinking deeply about, such as remembering how to brush your teeth.

LEARNT SKILLS

Procedural memory is the recall of how to perform an action or skill you have learnt in the past, such as mastering a swimming stroke or tying your shoelaces. It is an 'implicit' memory because you can perform the action or skill without having to think too deeply about it.

Semantic memory is the memory you use to store knowledge of the world. It contains your understanding of concepts, ideas, rules, facts and language. For example, your semantic memory would store the fact that the Eiffel Tower is in Paris.

The Eiffel Tower...   *is in Paris...*   *in France*

DISTANT MEMORY

Your memory is far from foolproof. Memories can fade over time, not be stored as you would like, or not be recalled as quickly and accurately as you need. You can even be tricked by suggestion into believing in memories that are not true or never happened.

INTERNAL JOURNAL

Episodic memory consists of memories of personal facts and events – your personal autobiography. These can range from places you have travelled to and the emotions you felt in certain situations, to recalling the name of your first pet or that you had eggs for breakfast.

53

SHORT TERM, LONG TERM

Your brain is equipped with a number of types of memory, including working memory, which is a space for processing information and calculations made by your brain, and short-term memory which keeps track of what's happening on a second-by-second basis

Short-term memory is a temporary storage locker for very recent experiences from your senses which, for a very brief moment, are stored in another type of memory called sensory memory. Once information leaves your sensory memory, it's gone and cannot be recalled unless it has been passed on to your short-term memory.

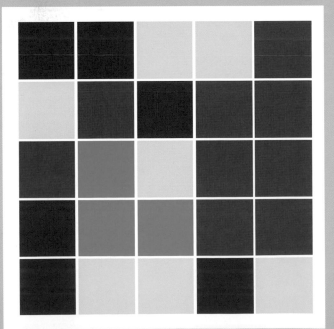

● 1. Data from your senses goes into your sensory memory, where it is held very briefly.

TESTING TIMES

You can test your short-term memory by staring at the square on the left for ten seconds. Now move a piece of paper so it covers the square and answer the questions on the opposite page.

54

USE IT OR LOSE IT

If you pay attention to data from your sensory memory, then chances are that data will go into your short-term memory. This memory has very limited capacity. In tests, psychologist George Miller concluded that a person's short-term memory could only hold around seven pieces of information, so with limited space, it needs a regular clear out. It's said that your short-term memory lasts around 15–20 seconds. If information in your short-term memory is not acted on in some way then it will disappear to make room for new information.

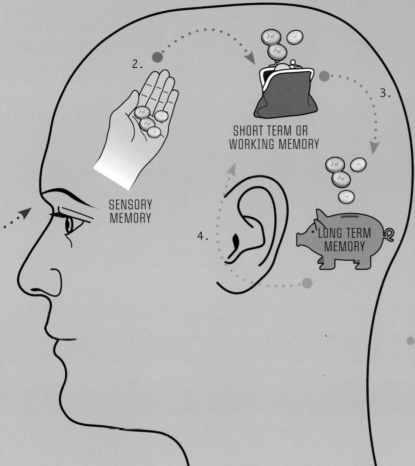

2. If you pay attention to the data, it goes into short-term memory.

SENSORY MEMORY

SHORT TERM OR WORKING MEMORY

LONG TERM MEMORY

3. If it is acted on in some way, the data is encoded into long-term memory.

4. From your long-term memory, the data can be retrieved back to your short-term or working memory.

MAKING MEMORIES

If your brain decides that something in your short-term memory is important to you then it will be encoded, meaning it will be processed into a form that allows it to be stored in your long-term memory. At a later point, this stored information can be retrieved. As far as we know, long-term memory can store unlimited amounts of information for as long as a person remains alive, even if retrieving a piece of information may not always be easy or possible.

>> MEMORY TEST QUESTIONS

1. Which colour appeared in the most squares?
2. Which colour appeared in the least number of squares?
3. What colours were the four corners of the square?

FORGOTTEN SOMETHING?

Can you remember the colour of the coin purse on the previous page, or how many coins were shown in the hand? Your memory may be good, but it may not always recall absolutely everything you would like it to.

There are lots of different ways you can test or exercise your memory — from trying to memorize a shopping list containing 12–25 items, to listening and repeating back a series of numbers with each series one digit longer.

TRAY TEST

You can test your short-term memory by performing this simple tray test. Stare at the tray of objects below for 45 seconds and then close the book. Now, write down all the objects you can remember. Once you've stopped writing, open the book to check. Did you recall them all? Try this test out on others and then attempt the second task. Covering up the large image below, look at the smaller tray at the top of page 57. Which items that were on the larger tray are not on the smaller one?

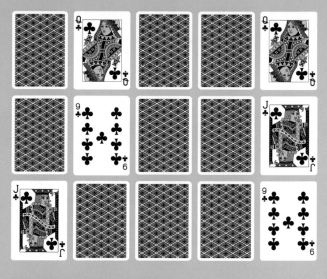

What object or objects are missing from this tray?

FIND THE PAIR

Another popular memory exercise is the card game 'Concentration', or 'Pairs'. Using the same twenty playing cards from two packs, shuffle the cards and place them face down in rows. Turn over two cards at a time trying to match pairs of the same card. If a match is made, leave those cards face up. If the two cards don't match, turn them back so they're face down and try again.

DRAWING ON YOUR MEMORY

Find out if you have a good memory for recalling visual detail by studying the shape, right, for 15 seconds. Then, close the book and try to draw the image from memory. How close were you? Many people get much of it right but end up drawing two pairs of circles and two sets of wavy lines without connecting the lines to the outer circles. You may find it helpful to count and name the different elements of the shape during the memorizing period.

MEMORY JOGGERS

Your memory often relies on association, linking different memories together so that when you recall one memory, it may remind you of another. These memories don't have to be of the same type. For example, when you recall several words to describe your favourite food, you may also summon up a memory of its taste or smell, or a visual memory of how it looks.

Associations can offer remarkable memory recall, but your brain doesn't always get the associations right and it can also be remarkably susceptible to suggestion. This can create memories of events and things that didn't really happen. These are known as false memories.

Elephants sniffing an orange

Ship about to hit a witch

Blish

Cend

DOODLES WITH A DIFFERENCE

These simple cartoons are a cross between a riddle and a doodle. People have to guess what the image is and the answer is often a joke. Look at these four pictures for 20 seconds – two with jokey titles and two with nonsense titles – then close the book and see if you can draw them from memory. Did you find the top two easier to remember and draw? This is because your brain finds it easier to memorize things that have labels or names that mean something to you, and harder to memorize things that do not.

List 1	List 2
egg	blanket
pillow	pillow
table	bed
walk	cosy
umbrella	dream
rocket	night
sleep	teddy
chair	awake
apple	light
dream	mattress

FALSE MEMORIES

Look at the two lists of words on the right, then close the book. Go and do something else for five minutes, then grab a pencil and paper and try to write down the words that appear in both lists. Now compare your answers: 'pillow' and 'dream' were in both lists, but did you include 'sleep'? It was only in List 1. Your brain has created a false memory influenced by all the sleep and bedroom-related words found in List 2.

What memories do you associate with a tennis ball?

BY ASSOCIATION

Associations may vary for different people based on their experiences and memories. The sight of a tennis ball can recall associations of summer for one person, including tennis, strawberries and summer rain. For another person who practised soccer with a tennis ball, it may prompt associations of sports halls, scoring a goal, or their favourite team or footballer. For a gardener who had a recent greenhouse window broken by a tennis ball, it may prompt other, less positive associations.

BRAIN CHANGE

Your brain doesn't stay the same. It booms in the womb, develops rapidly after you are born and continues changing throughout your life. Your prefrontal cortex, for example, doesn't mature until you're an adult. Your brain's ability to be shaped by experience and reorganize parts of itself, altering connections between different neurons, is known as brain plasticity.

As you grow older, the number of connections between neurons tends to fall, meaning that right now you are technically brainier than your parents! Tackling new tasks that test out different parts of your brain, such as learning to play a musical instrument or a new sport, or mastering a new skill such as juggling (see right), can be good mental exercise to keep your brain active and making new neural connections.

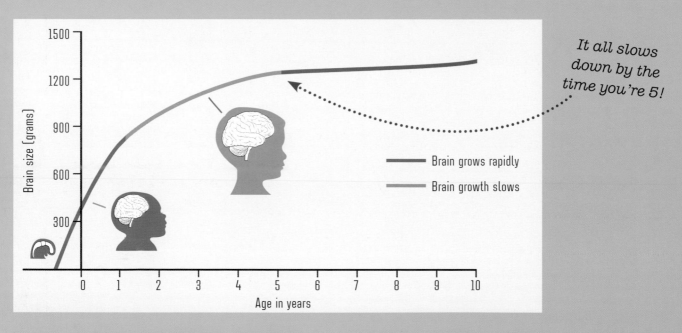

It all slows down by the time you're 5!

Brain grows rapidly
Brain growth slows

THE DEVELOPING BRAIN

The mighty human brain begins as a tiny hollow tube made from the skin of the embryo inside the mother's womb. At about 11 weeks, the cerebrum begins to expand and the brain starts to take shape. When born, a baby's brain has around the same number of neurons as an adult — around 100 billion — but the brain is only 300–400 grams in weight, about a quarter of an adult's brain. By the time a child is 3 years' old, the brain has packed on the weight as it produces thousands of billions of connections between its neurons. A 3-year-old's hippocampus matures as well, allowing the child to retain memories.

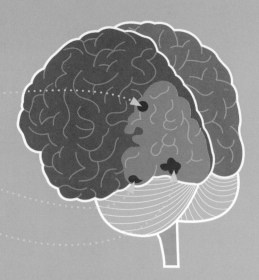

Keep on practising those juggling moves and you might just change your brain as a result! A University of Regensburg study performed three sets of brain scans on a group of people – before they learned to juggle, as soon as they had learned, and then three months after they had stopped juggling. It discovered that learning to juggle formed new connections and brain growth in several parts of the brain (see left). However the final scans, after the people had stopped juggling for three months, showed that their brains had largely returned to their previous pre-juggling state. So, when it comes to developing your brain, the message is clear: use it or lose it!

LEARN TO JUGGLE THREE BALLS

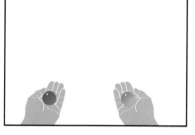

Hold your hands out in front of you at waist height, with a ball in each hand.

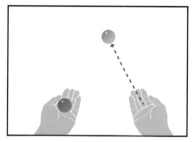

Swing your right hand inwards and throw the right ball up and over to a point above your left hand.

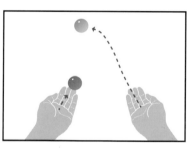

As the first ball peaks, throw the second ball to a similar point above your right hand.

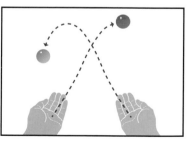

Repeat throwing and catching the two balls and as one ball lands, throw it back up and over again.

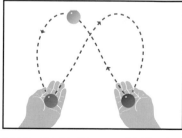

Add the third ball to your right hand. Throw the first ball up as you did before. As it peaks, throw your second ball.

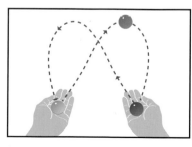

As the second ball peaks, throw the third. Keep throwing and catching and build a good rhythm.

GLOSSARY

brain plasticity
The ability of the brain to change and rewire itself during its life span.

central nervous system
The part of your nervous system made up of your brain and spinal cord.

cerebrum
The largest part of the brain, split into left and right halves, or hemispheres, and containing four lobes: the frontal, parietal, temporal and occipital lobes.

cognitive
Conscious processes your brain performs such as thinking, learning and remembering information.

cornea
The transparent front part of the eye that covers the iris and pupil.

EEG
Short for electroencephalogram, a procedure that uses electrodes on the scalp to record the electrical activity of neurons in the brain.

endocrine system
A system of different glands that produce chemicals called hormones, which help control and maintain many parts of your body.

hormones
Chemicals used by the endocrine system to transmit messages.

interpersonal intelligence
A person's ability to relate well to others, understand them and interact with them.

limbic system
A set of brain structures that help regulate emotions and are also important in learning and memory.

neurons
The technical term for nerve cells — specialized cells in the body that transmit signals in the nervous system.

neuroscientist
Scientists who specialize in the study of the brain and the nervous system.

neurotransmitters
Chemicals that act as messengers, helping to relay signals between nerve cells.

non-verbal communication
Ways of communicating without using speech, including the expressions you make, your posture and hand gestures.

optic nerve
Large bundles of nerve fibres which carry signals from your eyes to your brain for processing.

pain receptors
Specialized nerve cells which register different forms of pain, sending signals that travel to the brain.

perception
The ability to make sense of what one sees, hears, feels, tastes or smells.

photoreceptor cells
Specialized cells in the eyes, known as rods and cones, which convert light into electrical signals sent to your brain.

proprioception [pro-pri-o-cep-tion]
The sense that allows you to keep track of where all the parts of your body are at any given time.

Rapid Eye Movement [REM]
Periods of sleep when there is rapid movement of the eyes underneath the closed eyelids.

retina
The layer of light-sensitive cells that cover the back of the eye.

spinal cord
A thick bundle of nerve fibres that run through the spine from the base of the brain to the hip area.

synapse
A small gap between nerve cells across which signals can pass from one nerve cell to the next.

thalamus
Part of the brain which is involved in relaying signals from the senses to other parts of the brain. It also helps regulate sleep and alertness.

ANSWERS

p.34 MAGIC MISDIRECTION
Blind To Change In the second image the basketball is missing.

p.37 GUESSING GAMES
Seeking Out Patterns You should be able to see a standing dalmatian dog facing to the right.

pp.38—39 INTELLIGENT LIFE
Spatial Intelligence Pattern A makes the finished cube and pattern C makes the finished parallelogram.

Verbal Intelligence Here are 26 words you can make out of the word 'verbally':
a, able, ale, all, alley, bale, ball, bare, bay, bear, bell, blare, brave, by, label, lay, rally, rave, real, really, vale, valley, vary, verb, verbal, yell

p.41 LOGICAL THINKING
Numbers Game This is how you position the numbers 4 to 9 so that each side adds up to the same total (17):

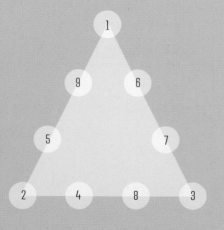

Thinking Out of the Box Ask the fruit stall owner to pick from the pineapple and bananas box. Since that box is labelled incorrectly, it can only contain one type of fruit, not two. So if he picks a pineapple, then you know that box must be pineapples. This means that the box marked bananas must be bananas and pineapples (because it can't be bananas), so the box marked pineapples must be bananas.

p.42 SOLVING PROBLEMS
Reasoning Riddles February is the month that people sleep the least as it has fewer days and nights than other months.

pp.48—49 SOCIAL ANIMALS
Body Language The person on the furthest right is displaying defensive body language.

Facing Up To Feelings The facial expressions are:

Unhappy

Happy

Suspicious

Shocked

Scared

Angry

INDEX

photo credits

p.2 © Betacam-S/Shutterstock.com; p.5 © Iynea/Shutterstock.com; p.6 © Eric Isselee/Shutterstock.com; p.7 © Skripnichenko Tatiana/Shutterstock.com; p.8 © wowomnom/Shutterstock.com; p.9 © Gordana Sermek/Shutterstock.com; p.9 © SerdarCelenk/iStock; p.9 © Bruce Rolff/Shutterstock.com; p.15 © Ollyy/Shutterstock.com; p.17 © Denis Kuvaev/Shutterstock.com; p.18 © Wellcome Dept. of Cognitive Neurologuy/Science Photo Library; p.19 © atipp/Shutterstock.com; p.19 © James King-Holmes/Science Photo Library; p.19 © Ganna Demchenko/Shutterstock.com; p.20 © Photostock-Israel/Science Photo Library; p.20 © Dudarev Mikhail/Shutterstock.com; p.21 © Eye of science/Science Photo Library; p.21 © Aspen Photo/Shutterstock.com; p.21 © B & T Media Group Inc./ Shutterstock.com; p.23 © Skripnichenko Tatiana/ Shutterstock.com; p.30 © pking4th/Shutterstock.com; p.31 © Matt_Brown/iStock; p.31 © Popartic/Shutterstock.com; p.31 © Zurijeta/Shutterstock.com; p.33 © Hidden Expedition: Smithsonian Hope Diamond, courtesy Big Fish and Eipix Entertainment; p.34 © efecreata mediagroup/Shutterstock.com; p.38 © duckycards/iStock; p.43 © Lewis Tse Pui Lung/Shutterstock.com; p.43 © Ana Blazic Pavlovic/Shutterstock.com; p.44 © Elnur/Shutterstock.com; p.44 © M. Unal Ozmen/Shutterstock.com; p.44 © Veronica Louro/Shutterstock.com; p.45 © Volodymyr Burdiak/Shutterstock.com; p.46 Image courtesy of PNAS and Lauri Nummenmaa, Enrico Glerean, Riitta Hari and Jari Hietanen, from the article: Bodily Maps of Emotions, PNAS, vol. 111, no. 2, January 14 2014, pp646-651; p.47 © Vladimir Gjorgiev/Shutterstock.com; p.47 © Sergiy Bykhunenko/Shutterstock.com; p.48 © badahos/Shutterstock.com; p.49 © drbimages/iStock; p.49 © Hans Kim/ Shutterstock.com; p.49 © mimagephotography/Shutterstock.com; p.49 © Wavebreak Media/Thinkstock; p.50 © Eric Isselee/Shutterstock.com; p.51 © Steve Mann/Shutterstock.com; p.51 © alex_187/Shutterstock.com; p.51 © Jorg Hackemann/Shutterstock.com; p.51 © Mogens Trolle/Shutterstock.com; p.51 © irabel8/Shutterstock.com; p.52 © S.Pytel/Shutterstock.com; p.53 © Yurkalmmortal/Shutterstock.com; p.53 © Andrei Marincas/Shutterstock.com; p. 53 © Artem Zhushman/Shutterstock.com; p.53 © Olesia Bilkei/Shutterstock.com; p.59 © DeanHarty/Shutterstock.com; p.59 © Kitch Bain/Shutterstock.com; p.59 © MaraZe/Shutterstock.com; p.59 © Iroom Stock/Shutterstock.com. All illustrations by John Woodcock, © Ivy Press 2015.